First Day Fright

BONNIE BADER AND TRACEY WEST
ILLUSTRATIONS BY ALBERT MOLNAR

D1310076

SCHOLASTIC INC.

New York   Toronto   London   Auckland   Sydney
Mexico City   New Delhi   Hong Kong

ISBN 0-439-21553-6

Text copyright © 2000 by Bonnie Bader and Tracey West
Illustrations copyright © 2000 by Scholastic Inc.

12 11 10 9 8 7 6 5 4 3 2 1   0 1 2 3 4 5 6/0

Printed in the U.S.A.
First Scholastic printing, October 2000

CONTENTS

CHAPTER ONE

Welcome to Second Grade

There is something spooky about my new school. I am not sure exactly what it is. My new school is just, well, different.

It all started on my first day. Dad drove me to the new school. My old school was a plain brown building.

Not this school. This school was painted bright orange. And I thought I saw bats flying around it. But then again, maybe they were just birds.

Dad dropped me off at the principal's office. My old principal always wore a blue suit. His office was very neat.

Not this principal. This principal, Dr. Beaker, had gray hair. It stuck straight up. He wore a white lab coat.

"Welcome to our school, Jane," Dr. Beaker told me. He walked back and forth as he talked. "I see you are in second grade."

Dr. Beaker told me how great the school was. I didn't listen. I couldn't take my eyes off the stuff in his room.

He had lots of glass cups and tubes lying around.

I saw something bubbling on a table behind him. I gasped. Lab coat. Tubes. Something bubbling. This man wasn't a principal. He was a mad scientist!

But then again, maybe he was only boiling water for coffee. Or tea.

"Let's get you to Ms. Batley's class," Dr. Beaker said.

He walked me to class. I wondered what my new teacher would be like. My old teacher had short blond hair. She wore colorful sweaters.

Not this teacher. This teacher, Ms. Batley, had long black hair. She had on dark red lipstick. She wore a black dress that touched the floor. A silver bat necklace hung around her neck.

"You must be Jane Plain," Ms. Batley said. "Welcome to our class. You are just in time for our snack."

Ms. Batley handed me a cup of red juice. I took the cup.

Then I looked at Ms. Batley again. Long black hair. Black dress. Bat necklace.

What if Ms. Batley was a vampire?

I looked at the juice again. Was it juice? Or was it blood? Vampires love to drink blood.

"No, thank you," I told Ms. Batley. "I'm not thirsty."

"Fine," Ms. Batley said. "Let me introduce you to your classmates."

I turned around and looked at the class. The kids in my old school wore dresses and jeans and T-shirts.

Not these kids.

A kid named Dave Draco smiled at me. He had on a black suit and a red bow tie. It looked like he had two pointy fangs.

Maybe he was another vampire. Or maybe he just needed to go to the dentist.

Then there was a girl named Glenda Specter. She had hair as white as snow. Her skin was so pale, I could almost see through it.

Maybe she was a ghost. Or maybe she just needed a little sun.

Wally Wolfson wore a long-sleeved shirt. I thought I saw fuzzy brown hair sticking out from under his sleeve.

Maybe Wally Wolfson was a werewolf. Or maybe he was just a very hairy boy.

Hazel Goodwitch had her dark hair in two long braids. She wore a black dress. Her black eyeglasses were shaped like cat eyes. A backpack shaped like a cat hung over her chair. And a broom was propped against her desk.

I bet you can guess what Hazel looked like. A witch, of course!

Or maybe she just really liked Halloween.

"You can sit behind Hazel," Ms. Batley told me.

I took my seat. The other kids finished their juice.

"Don't forget, we have a spelling test this afternoon," Ms. Batley said.

A spelling test? On my first day? I raised my hand.

"Yes, Jane?" Ms. Batley asked.

"Ms. Batley, I didn't study for a spelling test," I said. "Do I have to take it?"

Ms. Batley smiled. "Why, Jane, I'm surprised at you," she said. "Everyone knows how to spell. I'm sure you'll do just fine."

Hazel turned around and looked at me.

"I've been spelling since I could talk," Hazel said. "Haven't you?"

"Uh, sure," I lied.

But to myself, I thought, Hmmm. Hazel looked like a witch. And she was good at spelling. Witches. Spells.

What if the spelling test was a *magic* spelling test?

I did not want to find out. Maybe I could pretend I was sick. I started to raise my hand again.

But Ms. Batley was passing a jar around the class.

"It's time for our math lesson," she said. "Everyone, please take ten counters from the jar."

I put down my hand. Math was my best subject in my old school. I was good at using counters to solve math problems.

I tried to relax. I was probably just imagining that I saw witches, vampires, ghosts, and werewolves everywhere. I was just nervous about my first day of school.

Hazel passed the jar of counters to me. I looked in the jar.

It was filled with tiny black spiders!

I almost threw the jar on the floor. Then I looked again. The spiders were not moving. They were plastic spiders. Just toys. Nothing to be afraid of.

I reached into the jar. I counted out ten spiders.

I started to pass the jar to Dave Draco. Then I froze.

One of the spiders was crawling up my arm!

I dropped the jar. Spiders flew everywhere.

"*Eeeeeeeeeeek!*" I screamed.

CHAPTER TWO

Trapped!

The whole class turned and stared at me.

"Jane, whatever is the matter?" Ms. Batley asked. She ran over to my desk.

I felt my arm. There was nothing on it, except a loose thread from my T-shirt. I brushed it away. Then I looked down at the floor. The spiders were all over the place. The *plastic* spiders. What a mess! What was wrong with me today? And what was I going to tell Ms. Batley? How embarrassing!

"Uh — uh, I hurt my finger on the jar," I lied for the second time that day.

Some of the kids in the class started to giggle. I think they knew I wasn't telling the truth.

"Let me see," Ms. Batley said, lifting up my hand. "Is there any blood?" Her eyes lit up.

Blood? Oh, no! She wants my blood?

"No, no," I said, pulling my hand away. "I'm fine."

"Are you sure?" she asked. "Maybe you should go see the school nurse, Mrs. Frankie Stein. She's very good."

Did she just say *Frankenstein*? I didn't want to think about it. I just shook my head no.

After our math lesson, which was pretty normal, it was time for gym.

"Let's line up," Ms. Batley told us. "Now, don't forget, class. After gym you have lunch. And after lunch we have our spelling test."

I heard Hazel giggling with a few other girls. "I can't wait," Hazel said.

I can, I thought.

As we walked down the hall to the gym, I looked at the walls. In my old school, kids' work hung on the walls. Not in this school. In this school, the only things on the walls were pictures of people who had been principal of the school.

I looked at the pictures as we walked. There were lots of principals. This school must be really old, I thought. Finally, I saw a picture of Principal Beaker. Then I stopped in my tracks and gasped. Principal Beaker — the one in the picture, not the real one — winked at me! I was sure of it!

But before I had a chance to really think about it, I felt a sharp pain in my neck.

I quickly turned around. Dave Draco was in back of me. "Sorry," he said, smiling.

I stared at his fangs. Then I grabbed my neck. Had he just taken a bite out of me?

Then I noticed the pointy pencil in his hand. "I forgot to put this in my desk before we left," he said.

I breathed a sigh of relief. "Don't worry about it," I said. "I'm sorry I stopped so suddenly."

We finally reached the gym. In my old school, the gym had clean, shiny floors. Not this gym. This gym had black floors. They were very dusty. I even thought I saw spiderwebs hanging from the ceiling. I shivered. I didn't want to think about spiders again.

The gym teacher, Mr. Mumford, told us to sit down on the floor. In my old school, our gym teacher always wore shorts and a T-shirt. Not Mr. Mumford. He wore long white pants. And a white long-sleeved shirt. He had lots of white bandages all over him. On his face. On his neck. On his hands. In fact, he had so many bandages on that there wasn't a single bit of skin showing!

Maybe he was a mummy. Or maybe he had been in a bad accident.

Mr. Mumford told us we'd be working on gymnastics. I love gymnastics.

The class split up. I went with a group of kids over to the balance beam. Great! I was really good on the balance beam.

I stood in line behind Hazel. Wally Wolfson stood behind me.

Dave Draco went first. He climbed onto the beam. Then he took one careful step after another until he reached the end.

"Woooooooh!" cheered Wally.

I jumped. Wally's cheer sounded like a wolf's howl. But then again, maybe he just liked to cheer. A lot.

Soon it was Hazel's turn. She took a running start and then she *flew* up on the beam. I was sure of it!

"Woooooooh!" Wally howled again. He nudged me. "She really flew up there!"

I gulped.

"Come on, Jane," Hazel called out. "It's your turn."

I grabbed my stomach. "Uh, I'm not feeling so well," I lied for the third time that day.

"That's too bad," Hazel said, shaking her head. "The balance beam is loads of fun!"

I gave Hazel a little smile. "Maybe next time," I said.

Mr. Mumford blew a whistle. "Time to line up!" he called.

Glenda Specter ran up next to me. "Come on, Jane," she whispered in my ear. "We don't want to be late for lunch."

Then Glenda took my hand and pulled me toward the line.

Or at least I *thought* she took my hand.

The problem was I couldn't *feel* her holding my hand. See it, yes. But feel it, no way.

I looked at Glenda. Her white hair bobbed up and down as she ran. White hair. Pale skin. Just like a ghost. Yikes! I pulled my hand away.

Glenda stopped running. "What's wrong, Jane?" she whispered.

"Uh, I have to tie my laces. They feel loose," I lied for the fourth time that day.

Glenda shrugged. "Okay," she said.

I bent down to fix my laces. The rest of the class lined up and started to leave the gym.

I took a deep breath. I had to calm down. I was probably still nervous about my first day in a new school. I got up and ran to catch up with the rest of the class.

I ran out of the gym and looked down the hall. There, the class was just turning a corner. I could catch up with them in a second.

I ran around the corner. I didn't see the class. But I

did see that picture of Principal Beaker. The one I thought had winked at me before.

I ran on. Down the hall. Around another corner. Still no class.

Then I saw the picture of Principal Beaker again. This was strange. Was I running around in circles?

I ran down another hall. And another. And another. And each time I turned a corner, I saw that same picture of Principal Beaker. Again, and again, and again!

Oh, no! Not only was I lost, I was trapped. Trapped in school forever!

CHAPTER THREE

Freaky Food

"May I help you, Miss Plain?"

It was Principal Beaker's voice! The painting was talking to me!

I was so scared I couldn't move.

"Jane Plain, I asked you a question," Principal Beaker said sternly.

Then I realized. It wasn't the painting talking. It was the real Principal Beaker. He was standing behind me.

"Sorry," I said. "I'm lost. I need to find the lunchroom."

The principal smiled. "I'll show you the way," he said. "Next time, stick with the other students."

"Yes, sir," I said.

We turned a corner. There, plain as day, was a door marked CAFETERIA.

"Enjoy your lunch, Jane," Principal Beaker said.

I walked into the lunchroom.

Maybe there will be some normal kids in here, I

thought. Kids who don't look like vampires or ghosts. Maybe I can make some friends.

But everyone in the lunchroom looked a little strange to me. Lots of girls wore black dresses and carried broomsticks like Hazel. I saw another kid wrapped in bandages, just like Mr. Mumford.

A few boys were wearing purple shirts with stars and moons on them. Like wizards. One boy had a crow on his shoulder. Other kids were as pale as Glenda.

Hazel saw me. "Jane, come sit with us!" she called out.

I sighed. I might as well sit with Hazel and the others. They looked just as strange as everyone else. But at least they were being nice to me.

I sat down at a long table with Hazel, Dave, Wally, and Glenda.

Hazel swallowed a bite of sandwich. "So, how do you like our school?" she asked.

"It's, uh, different," I said. "My old school was a lot different."

"I thought all schools were the same," Glenda said in her soft, slow voice. "Nothing but homework, homework, homework."

"At least we have gym," Wally said. "And recess. I get to run around as much as I want."

Wally ran in circles around the table. The other kids laughed. Even I had to laugh. Wally was a pretty funny kid.

"What's your favorite subject?" Dave asked me.

"Math, I guess," I said.

Dave smiled. "I like math, too," he said. "My father is a great count. I guess it runs in the family."

I wasn't sure what Dave meant. But I smiled anyway. Dave was nice. All the kids were. I started to think I was wrong about them being — well, you know.

Then I noticed what they were eating.

Glenda had a plate of noodles from the cafeteria. At least I think they were noodles. They looked like they were moving!

Dave was slurping on some thick green soup. It smelled awful!

And Wally was eating some cookies. At least I think they were cookies. They looked a lot like dog biscuits to me.

"Jane, what did you bring for lunch?" Hazel asked me.

I opened my lunch box. Uh-oh. It was empty. My mom must have forgot to pack my lunch! "I don't have any," I said. My stomach growled.

All of the kids spoke at once.

"Have some of mine!" they said.

Glenda held out her plate of squiggly noodles. Dave held out a spoon of stinky soup. Wally held out a dog biscuit — I mean, cookie. And Hazel pulled out another sandwich from her bag. I guess she ate a lot.

I was hungry. And I didn't want to be rude. Hazel's sandwich looked like the safest bet.

"I guess I'm in a sandwich mood today," I said. "Thanks, Hazel."

I took the sandwich. It looked pretty normal. It smelled fine. It didn't feel like it was moving.

I took a deep breath. Then I took a bite.

"Eeeeeeeeeeeek!"

It wasn't me screaming this time.

It was the sandwich!

CHAPTER FOUR
The SPELLing Test

A screaming sandwich? Was it alive?!

"Eeeek!" Now *I* was screaming. I dropped the sandwich.

Hazel, Dave, Wally, and Glenda stared at me.

"What's wrong, Jane?" Hazel asked. She had a hurt look on her face. Like she was upset that I didn't like her sandwich.

"I — I thought I saw a bug. Crawling on the table," I lied again.

Wally jumped up from his seat. "A bug? Where?" His mouth began to water and he ran in circles.

I buried my head in my hands.

"Phew!" Hazel said. "It's only a bug. Don't worry, Jane. Wally will take care of it. He loves bugs. I'm just glad it wasn't my sandwich. I thought you didn't like it or something. After all, scream cheese sandwiches are my favorite. Don't you like them?"

Did Hazel just say *"scream* cheese"? I looked at the sandwich that was on the table. It looked like a normal cream cheese sandwich to me. Maybe that's what Hazel had said — *cream* cheese. It was awfully noisy in the lunchroom.

I reached for the sandwich. I was going to give it another try. But just as I was about to take another bite, the bell rang. Saved! Time to go back to class!

I wrapped up the sandwich in a napkin and threw it into the garbage.

Ms. Batley came to pick us up from the lunchroom.

"I can't wait for the spelling test!" Hazel said as we walked back to the classroom. "It's going to be the best one yet!"

What did Hazel mean by that? I didn't want to know.

Suddenly, I felt a cold breeze on my arms. I jumped. But it was only Glenda standing next to me.

"Hazel loves spelling tests, but I don't," Glenda whispered in my ear.

"Why not?" I asked.

"Well, you know," Glenda began, "we are not good at spelling. Not like Hazel."

What did she mean by "we"? I didn't want to ask.

Back in the classroom, Ms. Batley told us to clear our desks and take out a pencil. Then she passed out paper to the class.

I picked up my pencil. My hand started to shake. Why was I so nervous? It was just a plain old spelling test, after all. Wasn't it?

Ms. Batley gave us the first word: "zipping." *Zipping?* As in zipping your zipper? Or in zipping your lips? That was a strange spelling word. But I knew how to spell it.

"The next word is 'zooming,'" Ms. Batley said.

"I knew it!" Hazel whispered.

Why did Hazel say that, I wondered? At my old school, we always knew what words were going to be on the spelling test. That was because we *studied* for the test. Maybe Hazel hadn't studied.

The next few words were easy, too: ever, near, flapping, flying, and coming.

"The last word is 'here,'" Ms. Batley said.

I raised my hand. "Ms. Batley, could you use that word in a sentence, please?" I wasn't sure if she meant *hear*, like what you do with your ears, or *here*, like "here at this place." At my old school, my teacher always used the spelling words in a sentence.

"Why would you want me to do that?" Ms. Batley asked.

I blushed. "Because I don't know which word you mean."

I heard some of the kids giggle.

"Come on, Jane!" Hazel shouted out. "We're all waiting!"

Waiting for what? I wondered. I didn't want to ask.

I took a guess and wrote down h-e-r-e.

Suddenly, I heard a loud noise. It sounded almost like bird wings flapping. Only louder. But it couldn't be, could it?

I looked up. In through the window flew a big brown bat! I started to scream. So did the rest of the class. Or were they cheering? I couldn't tell. The bat swooped down near me. *Eeeek!* I buried my head in my arms.

Then the room got quiet. No more flapping. Or screaming. Or cheering. Slowly, I lifted up my head. Ms. Batley was standing in front of the class with a big smile on her face. "Excellent job, class!"

An excellent job on what? I wondered. On the spelling test? I looked down at the words and read them to myself: *Zipping, zooming, ever, near, flapping, flying, coming, here.*

The words rhymed! Just like a spell! I read the words again. *Zipping, zooming, flapping, flying.* The words described a bat!

Oh, my gosh! Did we cast a spell to make a bat appear? I didn't want to think about it. Quickly, I passed my paper to the front of the class.

"I told you spelling was fun," Hazel whispered to me.

Ms. Batley was very pleased with the spelling test. She gave us free time to write in our journals.

Soon, the bell rang. I lined up with the other kids. On the way out, Ms. Batley smiled.

"I hope you enjoyed your first day of school, Jane," Ms. Batley said.

"Of course," I said. But inside, I wasn't so sure.

Was my teacher a vampire? Were my new friends monsters? Was the principal a mad scientist?

Maybe they were. Or maybe I was just imagining things.

"See you tomorrow, Jane," called out Hazel, Dave, Wally, and Glenda.

Tomorrow?

How could I survive another day in this spooky school?